# THE BEST DAD

Based on the TV series *Angela Anaconda*®
created by Joanna Ferrone and Sue Rose as seen on the Fox Family Channel®

SIMON SPOTLIGHT
An imprint of Simon & Schuster Children's Publishing Division
1230 Avenue of the Americas, New York, New York 10020

Manufactured in the United States of America

First Edition
2  4  6  8  10  9  7  5  3  1

ISBN 0-689-84039-X

Library of Congress Control Number 00-111808

{family}

# Angela Anaconda™

## THe BEST DaD

adapted by Laura McCreary
and Mark Myers

based on the scripts by
Charlotte Fullerton and Mark Myers

illustrated by Barry Goldberg

Simon Spotlight

New York    London    Toronto    Sydney    Singapore

# Story Number One

# BIG HOEDOWN

# CHAPTER ONE

My dad, Bill, is the most perfect dad in the world. He's a salesman, and he's also an inventor, and one day he'll combine his two jobs and sell one of his inventions. Until then, I'm happy just having him around, inventing cool stuff that helps around the house.

But I have to tell you that today my dad is not so perfect, on account of he has entered us in a square-dancing contest, for square dancers.

When my dad pulls the car into the Spangly Jangles parking lot and tells me to "Giddyap, partner," I sink further down into my seat, hoping that no one sees me.

Once we're in the store we start trying on "duds," which is what Dad calls them, which is what I really think they are: "duds." And the worst part is that they are matching duds, as in we're both wearing the same ugly plaid shirt!

Right in the middle of our Western wear modeling session, Spangly Jangles himself comes over. "Yee-haw! Blamed if it ain't ol' cowboy Bill himself!"

Dad and Spangly shake hands. On account of they're friends, 'cause Dad sold Spangly a mechanical bull last year.

"How's she doing?" Dad asks, pointing to the electric bucking bronco across the room.

"She's still a-buckin' like a pony in a

poppycock coop," says Spangly, "and the best part is I don't ever have to feed her."

Then Spangly does one of the coolest things I've ever seen. He spits a gigantic spit right through a big gap in his front teeth. It flies across the room and lands in a silver spittoon with a *ding!* I'm beginning to think that maybe this Spangly is a real cowboy, on account of who else but a real cowboy would spit like that?

"Well, sir, I kin see y'all have mighty fine taste in Western duds, yessir," Spangly says, patting Dad on the shoulder. Then he turns to me. "And I got just the thang fer you, little buckaroo."

Spangly ducks into a back room and comes back with a pair of shiny metal spurs. He puts them on my heels, and I take 'em for a test spin. *Ching, ching, ching!* My spurs actually *ching* every time I take a step. Maybe

this hoedown idea is not such a bad idea after all!

"Now you'll be square dancing with the best of 'em," says Spangly.

"Oh, you'll be square dancing with the best, all right, Angela Anaconda," says a voice from behind me. I turn around and see that the voice is coming from exactly who I was hoping it wasn't coming from—my most hated enemy who I hate the most, Nanette Manoir!

# CHAPTER TWO

Just when something that wasn't supposed to be fun was starting to be fun, Ninnie Poo shows up! And what makes matters worse is she's with her father, who thinks he is a real cowboy.

"Howdy, you-all," he says. Anyone knows a real cowboy would say "y'all" instead of "you-all," which proves he's about as much a cowboy as Nanette Manoir is French, which is not at all.

"We're here to purchase a whole 'passel,' as they say, of Western wear to donate to the less fortunate participants in this year's hoedown," Nanette's father says, grabbing an armload of studded shirts marked 80 percent off.

"You aren't actually going to wear that *faux* turquoise bolo tie are you, ol' chap?" Mr. Manoir asks, tugging on Dad's new tie.

Dad takes back his bolo tie and changes the subject by asking Mr. Manoir about his business.

"Business is booming as usual," says Mr. Manoir. Then the mechanical bull across the room must have caught his eye, because Mr. Manoir mentions the bull my father sold him six months ago.

Mr. Manoir says he can't remember paying it off and asks Dad to send him a bill for whatever he owes and a receipt. "I'm donating the bull to the hoedown. I need the receipt for the tax write-off, you understand."

I hope my dad understands, 'cause I sure don't.

"Of course, the real big hit of the hoedown will be my cactus flower and me do-si-do-ing our way to yet another square-dance victory," Mr. Manoir says, patting his cactus flower—otherwise known as Ninnie-Pinhead Manoir—on the head.

"What will that make it, Daddy?" asks Nanette. "Two years in a row?"

Two years in a row that you have been an annoying un-French loser, I think.

Mr. Manoir smiles smugly. "Actually, cactus, after we win this year, we'll have three victories under our cowboy belts."

"I wouldn't be clearing a space for that trophy just yet," Dad says, saving the day like he usually does. "Angela and I are entering the competition this year, and we might just give you a run for your money."

Nanette turns to her dad, all full of fake smiles. "Daddy," she coos, "if the Anacondas are going to be in this year's hoedown, oughtn't we buy Angela a proper Western outfit? After all, we *are* donating Western wear to the less fortunate participants."

Nanette points to my socks, which are sagging. "And look, Angela Anaconda's socks are *so* old, they keep falling down into her boots!"

I'm about to tell Nanette that the reason my socks keep falling is because they want to get as far away from her ugly face as much as I do, when Dad steps in.

"I'm sure Nanette knows her offer is entirely unnecessary," Dad says.

"C'mon, Bill," says Mr. Manoir. "It's not

like your daughter couldn't use some sprucing up. After all, she's not going to get noticed for her dancing."

Suddenly Dad's eyes narrow, and his face gets red. "That does it, Howell!" he yells. "You can insult my business, you can even insult my bolo, but nobody insults my daughter's do-si-do! Nobody! I challenge you to a hoedown showdown."

Mr. Manoir and my dad stare at each other for a long time. If it *really* were the Old West and they really were cowboys, I bet they'd have their hands on their holsters. Then Mr. Manoir reaches into his pocket, and for a second I think that maybe he does have a holster, but instead he just pulls out a big wad of cash.

"Why don't we make it a little more interesting, shall we?" Nanette's dad says, waving dollars in our faces. "Say, if we win, I

won't have to pay you the money I owe on that mechanical bull you sold me."

"Okay," says Dad, "but if we win, you'll have to buy ten more bulls from me! Deal?"

"Deal!" answers Mr. Manoir. "And may the squarest dancer win."

# CHAPTER THREE

So now it is up to my dad and me to practice like we've never practiced before, which is a lot, on account of we haven't ever practiced before. We have to learn how to square-dance in time for the hoedown showdown.

Luckily, Dad has bought a practice tape with a practice announcer calling square-dancing steps for us to practice to. Only, now I realize that not only do we have to dance along to what the announcer says, we

have to dance along in rhyming dance steps. Whoever thought up square dancing must have thought about it a little too hard, because that's what it is—too hard!

"Swing your partner, do-si-do. Allemande left, to and fro," calls the announcer in a country twang. Dad and I try to do these things, except that when I go "to," he goes "fro," and we end up on the floor.

"Skip to my Lou, don't step on her toes. Promenade and round she goes." But step on my toes is exactly what he does.

"Sashay left an' sashay right. Swing your partner with all yer might," says the announcer. And Dad and I are starting to get it right! But just as he is about to swing me around, my socks fall down, and I have to stop do-si-do-ing and pull them up.

"Hold it right there, angelfish," says Dad. "I have just the thing to make those saggy socks a thing of the past." Then he pulls a pair of cowboy boots out of a bag.

"Cowboy boots?" I ask.

"Not just any cowboy boots," says Dad. "Cowboy boots with my patented sock-lock system. They have supersticky double-sided tape inside to stick to your socks so they won't sag ever again."

I pull on the boots and the best part is, they actually work like they're supposed to work. Dad has done it again!

"Those Manoirs don't stand a chance," says Dad, and I am beginning to think that he is right.

# CHAPTER FOUR

Dad and I are dressed in matching Western shirts that match, and I am wearing my sock-lock boots. We are ready as ready can be for the hoedown showdown.

We get to the hoedown extra early to pick out an extra-good dancing spot, but we aren't the only ones who are early. Nanette Manoir and her dad are already there warming up. And, can you believe it—they've brought along a dancing coach!

"Hello, Angela Anaconda. I'd like you to meet Pierre, our world-renowned choreographer who Daddy hired to help us perfect our already near perfect square-dancing moves," Nanette says as she shows off her do-si-dos.

And then I hear a huge "YEE-HAW!" from across the room and turn and see Spangly Jangles himself!

"Spangly!" I say. "Did you come to watch us dance the square dance?"

"Mr. Jangles is one of the judges of tonight's contest," Nanette's dad explains as he slips Spangly a big fat check with lots of big fat zeros. "Here," he says, "for all those duds I bought from you for the less fortunate."

"Woo-wee," Spangly says, pocketing the check, "you just kept me in business for the next ten years!"

But so what if Spangly Jangles votes for

the Man-Worms on account of they bought a lot of duds? Dad says it is the square-dance caller who can make you or break you. And if I were Ninnie Poo, I would prepare to be broken!

Just then the square-dance caller steps up to the microphone, and it's the same Pierre who had coached the Man-Cheaters all of last week! "Didn't I tell you?" says Nanette. "Daddy is also donating the square-dance caller."

And before I can yell that that is unfair, Pierre starts calling, so we have to start dancing.

"It's contest time, so if you dare, grab your partners and form a square," says Pierre. "Allemande left and do a twist, do-si-do around like this. All join hands, raise up to the middle, hands out front like cakes on the griddle."

Dad and I start dancing, and we are actually not bad. We are allemande-ing, do-si-do-ing, and hand-joining better than just about anyone, and definitely better than Nanette and her un-cowboy father. And Nanette knows it, 'cause the next thing she does is wink at Pierre.

"Mix it up, Pierre," she says, and Pierre actually winks back, which is how I know that Dad and I are about to be in trouble.

"Switch your partner! Don't be shy! Time to dance with the other gal's guy!" Pierre calls.

Nanette grabs my dad, and Nanette's dad grabs me, and before we know it they are spinning us around and around until I am more dizzy than I've ever been in my short life.

"Now that you have got the knack, find your partner, switch them back," calls

Pierre. Dad and I somehow stumble back to each other and immediately fall down on the ground. And the worst part is, while my dad and I are still trying to get up, Nanette and her dad are winning the contest right out from under us! Nanette grabs the trophy from the judges.

"My, my, my," says Nanette's dad. "It's even bigger than last year's—and the year before that!"

"Maybe next year there will be someone who's a worthy square-dance competitor instead of just a square," Nanette says, looking right at me.

# CHAPTER Five

Suddenly my brain can't take it anymore, and I am about to explode. Think of something to make yourself feel better, I think to myself. So, this is what I think:

Next time there is a square-dance competition, I will call the moves. And when I am a square-dance caller, Nanette will not be winning, I can promise you that, on account of she will have to do everything exactly as I tell her.

Are you ready, Little Nin? 'Cause my square dance will go a little something like this:

"Swing your partner, stub your toes, put your fingers up your nose."

Ninnie will clutch her painful foot in pain, but now is no time to stop dancing, on account of I am only getting started.

"Skip to my Lou, right down in the dumps. Look out! You're dancing in cow-pie clumps."

How does that smell, Nanette Manure? Sure doesn't smell like you'll win this showdown.

"Do-si-do with the mechanical bull, you'll never come off when sticky-tapes pull!"

That's right, Ninnie-Loser, you'll finish this dance on the bucking bronco! But it will buck you right out the door as I finish my square-dance calling:

"The winner of this hoedown is my dad and me. But you'll be too far away to see! The mechanical bull bucks you away, and I'll *take my trophy 'cause I won today!"*

Suddenly I hear Nanette yelling, "Don't touch it! You'll smudge the shine," and I realize that I'm accidentally holding the trophy.

"That's as close as you're ever going to get to winning a trophy, Angela Anaconda," Ninnie declares, yanking the trophy away from me.

"And that's as close as you'll ever be to getting paid for that mechanical bull," Mr. Manoir adds, laughing at my dad.

But Dad smiles, and I am thinking that maybe he has an idea. He turns to Spangly and says, "Hey, Spangly, don't you think the crowd should give the winners a big ol' Western 'hats off'?"

Dad takes his hat off and begins waving it at the Manoirs like he's actually glad they won. I can't believe my eyes!

"Dad, what are you doing?" I whisper.

"Trust me, angelfish," he says, still waving his hat.

Then Spangly grabs the microphone from Pierre. "Hey, folks," he says, "whadda y'all say we give a big ol' Western cheer for the winners?" Spangly takes off his cowboy hat and waves it in the air, yelling, "Yee-haw," and everyone does the same thing.

The Manoirs look at each other and realize that the only polite thing to do is wave back. And we all know how polite they have to be. So they try to take off their hats, but for some *strange* reason, the hats won't come off!

I look over at Dad, and he is actually snickering. "I had some supersticky double-sided tape left over from those boots I fixed for you, and I didn't want it to go to waste, so . . ."

"Yee-OUCH!" yells Nanette. "My hair! My hair!" I look to see that Ninnie's hat is stuck to her bologna hair, and she can't get it off. And then Mr. Manoir tugs at his hat with all his might, and suddenly his toupee pulls right off of his head, and he's standing there bald!

"See, angelwings?" Dad says as he winks my way. "I told you the father-daughter hoedown would be fun."

So, like I said, my dad is the most perfect dad in the world.

# Story Number Two

# GONE FISHING

# CHAPTER ONE

The only good thing about school is the school bell—well, that and lunch. And recess. And days when I get to run the slide projector and Nanette Manoir does not.

But right now, all I care about is waiting for the bell, on account of as soon as it rings, it's Friday afternoon, and Friday afternoon means tomorrow is Saturday morning, and on Saturday morning I get to go fishing with my dad.

When the bell finally rings, I hurry home from school and find my mom in the kitchen, making lunches for us to take on our trip. That's when I ask to help out, on account of right now the only person with her is my baby sister, Lulu, and I really don't think she's much help.

Mom and I have the sandwich-making going perfectly perfect (she's in charge of meat and cheese, and I'm in charge of mustard and mayonnaise), when my stupid brothers Mark and Derek come in and ruin it.

Did I tell you that Mark and Derek are going with us tomorrow? Probably not, on account of that's a fact I would like to forget. Mark reaches for a sandwich, and I slap his hand. "Those are for tomorrow," I tell him.

Then Mark tries to grab another sandwich, but Derek grabs it first.

"Hey!" Mark says, looking like he's gonna sock Derek in the face, and I hope he does, 'cause then they'll get grounded and they won't be able to go fishing tomorrow. "You ate that whole sandwich in one bite! You rock!"

That's when I leave the kitchen because I can't think about anything that I care about less than how Mark and Derek eat like pigs.

I walk into the garage and find my dad, who is hunched over working on something. When he looks up, I see that he has his heavy-duty welding mask on.

"Hi, angelfish," he says. "You'll never guess what invention I'm working on for tomorrow's fishing trip!"

# CHAPTER TWO

Dad shows me the coolest thing I've seen since he showed me his last cool invention. "Behold the Whirl-O'-Reel!" Dad says, holding it up.

I take a good look at the Whirl-O'-Reel. It looks like a regular fishing pole, only the bottom of it is full of gears and buttons—even more than a regular fishing pole is full of gears and buttons. I reach out to take it, but Dad yanks it away.

"Don't touch it! It's still molten," Dad warns. "Besides, before you learn to use the Whirl-O'-Reel, you've got to learn to fish! We'll just let this thing cool off."

Dad sets the Whirl-O'-Reel on a shelf, grabs two fishing poles from the corner, and walks out to the front yard.

"You know what they say," says Dad. "Give a man a fish and he'll eat for a day. Teach a man to fish and he'll eat for a lifetime. Now, here's how you cast."

Dad swings back his pole and lets the fishing line fly. It sails up, floating down gracefully and landing clear across the lawn.

"You try," Dad says, handing me the pole. I take the pole, swing it back, and let go— and the fishing line immediately gets caught in the bushes behind me.

"Takes practice," says Dad.

So we practice, and practice, and practice,

and by the time Mom calls us to dinner, I am casting so well that I've caught six flowers, two clumps of grass, and an entire mailbox.

During dinner, Dad says I'll soon be ready to be introduced to the Whirl-O'-Reel. "Your old man has almost finished the most amazing invention since the Pocket Fisherman. It reels in even the feistiest fishes with one tap of a button."

"If you can catch fish just by tapping a button, how come I just spent three hours learning how to cast a pole and wearing out my arm?" I ask.

"That's life, angelfish," replies Dad.

I ask him if I can stay up and help him perfect the Whirl-O'-Reel, but Dad says that I should get some sleep on account of tomorrow morning's going to be an early one.

# CHAPTER THREE

I'm in the middle of dreaming that I'm a world-famous fisherman, when my dad wakes me up. I hop out of bed already ready to go, on account of I put on my rubber wading pants the night before.

"Is it time for fishing?" I ask, but then Dad holds up his hands to show me that they're both all bandaged up in big white bandages!

"Uh, there's been a slight change of

plans," explains Dad. "My Whirl-O'-Reel was a little feisty. When I finished tweaking it, I took it for a test spin. The Whirl-O'-Reel caught a tire and reeled it right back into my hands. I'm afraid they're not quite fit for fishing. But don't you worry, angelfish, you're still going fishing. Your big brothers Mark and Derek are taking you. Isn't that great?"

I just stare at my dad, too shocked to speak. I guess he thinks that means yes, on account of the next thing he does is pat me on the head with his swollen hand and tells me he's glad I'm not disappointed.

NOT DISAPPOINTED? To have to go fishing with my dueling dumbbell brothers and not Dad? Not disappointed that I won't be able to try the Whirl-O'-Reel?

Oh, well, I do my best to try to smile so Dad doesn't feel bad.

We pile into Mark and Derek's car, and I'm beginning to think that fishing with my brothers might not be so horribly horrible after all, seeing as fishing with two morons is better than not fishing at all.

Once we pull up to the dock, Mark and Derek order me out of the car to buy supplies.

"If I'm getting the supplies, what are you two gonna do?" I ask.

"Arm wrestle . . . duh," Mark says.

And if it's not bad enough that my butthead brothers are ruining my day, up walks Nanette Manoir, who cuts in front of me at the bait shop.

"Well, well. Look what washed ashore. Going fishing, I see, Angela Anaconda? I also plan to have a voyage at sea. And I'd invite you to join me, but we don't allow riffraff aboard my *yacht*, which is French for '*expensive* boat'."

"I was here first," I tell Nanette.

Nanette pays no attention and orders something called sushi, which she calls a gourmet lunch, but I call raw fish that people eat raw! It turns out that the bait shop is also a sushi restaurant on account of they sell the good pieces of fish to people like Nanette to eat. Then they sell the fish insides and yucky parts to people like me for fishing.

"I was here first," I tell the lady who's working at the counter, "and I want some worms."

"Yes, yes," says Nanette, "but your worms can wait and my sushi cannot." Nanette grabs a container from the old lady. "Charge it to my account," she says as she walks out like someone who thinks she is important but actually is not.

"Have fun on your yuck-yacht!" I call

after Nanette not loud enough for her to hear me.

"And don't worry about me, because pretty soon I'm going to be knee-deep in fish up to my knees. My own fish that I caught myself which I even plan to cook myself so it will be cooked and not RAW!"

# CHAPTER FOUR

Mark and Derek and I finally get everything, including ourselves, into the boat.

"Well," I ask, "what first?"

"ROW!" they tell me as they each hand me an oar.

"The best fishing's at the center of the lake," Derek explains as he pops open a can of root beer. "So row!" Mark nods, taking the can from Derek.

"But how come I have to do all the

rowing and you guys don't?" I ask.

"Duh," says Derek, "so *we* can do all the fishing."

"You didn't think you were actually going to fish, did you?" adds Mark.

So for the next two hours I row the boat, put lures on Mark's and Derek's hooks, and I even have to climb a tree to untangle Mark's fishing line. And to make bad matters worse, Nanette Manoir keeps skiing by in her fancy un-French boat, splashing water on me. She thinks she's so great just because she can put two sticks on her feet and be pulled around on top of the water.

And meanwhile, Mark and Derek haven't even caught one fish, on account of they're using fake plastic lures in the shape of glittery fish with feathers on them—like any real fish would ever be dumb enough to eat those!

Finally Mark and Derek decide that their fancy lures must be too good for the fish in this lake, and they tell me to break out the worms. Only, now I can't find the container I got from the bait lady on account of the boat is so full of Mark's and Derek's empty soda cans.

"No worms, no fish," says Derek. "Angela, pass me a root beer. Fishing's over."

"OVER!" I exclaim. "After all this rowing and untangling and being splashed by Nanette Manoir, you're just going to quit fishing when you haven't even caught a single fish?"

Mark and Derek look at each other and nod. "Yeah," Mark says, "totally. Now, rest your arms. We need you to row back later."

And as Mark and Derek are laughing, and I am thinking that things can't get any worse, Nanette skis by one more time.

"Well, if it isn't Angela Angler-conda," she says. "What's the matter? I don't see any fish in your boat. I guess you've been too busy rowing to catch anything. Ever heard of something called a motor? My yacht has six of them!"

Then Alfredo revs up their motors, and they drench me with a big wave of water.

"Ever hear of something called a brain?" I call after her, but she's already skied off to ruin someone else's day.

# CHAPTER FIVE

So now I am looking at the bright sun shining down on the glittery water, and I am thinking to myself that the next time I go fishing, things will be very different. And a lot more fun. My bumbling brothers won't be bosses of the boat when I have things my way.

*First of all, there will be a nasty lake monster on the loose.*

*"Look out!" I will warn my brothers, but it*

will be too late, 'cause the nasty lake monster will flip the boat and send my brothers tumbling into the water.

"Never fear, my sunken siblings," I will tell them, "I'll save you!" Because, as Dad promised, I am the first to use the Whirl-O'-Reel! Then I will charge in on a sea horse, twirling my Whirl-O'-Reel like a lasso, cowboy-style.

Just as the lake monster is about to bite down on my brothers, I will cast the Whirl-O'-Reel and catch Mark and Derek by their feet, saving them from the jaws of the lake monster. But as I swing my brothers around my head, they will get caught up in seaweed and be wrapped up tight like sushi. Then I will serve my freshly rolled brothers to Nannoying Manoir, who I'm sure will find them very tasty!

Next I will hook Nanette and the sticks on

her feet to the back of my boat, and she will water-ski from behind it with my bite-size seaweed brothers. "Perhaps you'd enjoy some fast food . . . ," I will tell Nanette as I go faster and faster.

"Lucky for you, Ninnie Wart, this boat has a motor, which is French for 'You're going into a tree!'" Then I will make a very sharp turn and send Nanette smack into the tallest swamp tree, and my brothers will go flying through the air . . . never to be heard from again!

It makes me laugh just thinking about it. But then I remember that I am not in charge of the boat today and my brothers have not flown through the air, never to be heard from again.

Well, I think to myself, I think it's time for them to hear that enough is enough on account of I have had enough.

"I'm sick of you two being bosses of the boat," I tell them. "You're gonna listen to me for a change. I came here to fish, not to row or open root beers. So move over, my Neanderthal brothers, on account of I, Angela, your sister, have got some fish to catch!"

And my brothers don't say a word, on account of they are both sleeping. Sleeping? Thinking that I finally worked up the nerve to yell at them and they slept through the whole thing makes me so mad that I kick their mountain of soda cans. *Wham!*

The soda cans roll all over the boat, and then I see something. There it is, peeking out from under a couple of candy bar wrappers— the white container from the bait shop!

"The bait," I say as I quickly sneak the pole out of Mark's hand and dip the hook in the bait container. I cast out, and before you can say "Angela Anaconda is the best fisherman in the world," I hook a fish! Not just any fish, a giant fish. I need all my strength to reel it in and haul it into the boat.

I guess all my reeling and pulling and fish-catching must have been pretty noisy, 'cause Mark and Derek, who can sleep through a volcano erupting, wake up just as I hold up my trophy fish.

"Hey, check out that fish!" says Mark.

"Whoa," Derek adds, grabbing the fish from me, "I must have caught it while I was sleeping!"

Then Mark butts in and says, "No way, dude! I caught it while I was sleeping!"

"Angela caught it while you were both sleeping!" says a familiar voice. I look to the shore and see Dad, waving his bandaged hands that aren't bandaged anymore!

"Is there room for one more?" he asks. Dad explains that he iced his hands all day, and the swelling is down enough to hold a pole. "But I don't think I'd be much good at rowing."

I smile and tell Dad that I can handle the rowing part on account of I've had lots of practice at it. And I row to shore faster than I've ever rowed anywhere before!

Dad gets on the boat and admires the fish I caught. Derek stares at it, pouting. "I don't understand how you caught a fish without any bait," says Derek.

"I don't understand how you caught a fish at all," adds Mark.

"It was easy," I tell them, holding up the container I found, "on account of I actually found the bait."

Dad takes the container from me. He opens the lid and sniffs inside. Then he does something that shocks all of us. He actually takes out a piece of the bait I used and EATS IT!

"Dad! What are you doing? You can't eat that!" I cry.

"Actually, I can, angelfish. It seems the bait that you found is high-quality fresh sushi."

"But, if that's sushi, what happened to the worms I bought?" I ask, totally confused.

Just then Nanette Manoir's motorboat motors past us. "Pass the sushi, Alfredo," we hear her say. "It's time for lunch."

And you can imagine what happens next. Nanette lets out a scream to beat all screams: "WOOOORRRRRMMMMMSSSS!"

Dad smiles and holds up my huge fish. "Do you think we should share some of our lunch with her?"

And we both laugh so hard that we almost sink the boat.

# The End